Girl With A
Broken Heart

(A Book of love and gratitude)

Published By

Girl With A Broken Heart

Edited by Ilma Khan

Copyright ©

POETRY WORLD ORG 2020

ISBN (Paperback) - 9789389959512

First Edition : 2020

Book Design by POETRY WORLD

Girl With A Broken Heart

(A Book of love and gratitude)

Compiler

ILMA KHAN

Ilma Khan is a 17-year-old girl. She is in High School. She belongs to Rampur, UP. She is a writer, co-author of 30+ books, and author of *Unfiltered Saga of Love*. She is a well-known author.

Instagram. (@its_ilmakhan_)

Feel Him Forever

When You Are in Love with Someone, You Cannot Feel for Any Other Person.

Hey Zayn,

What's up dear?

I'm fine you tell!

I am fine.

Zayn, what about the question that was asked by Mitashi?

Zayn replied, "Which question?"

Arey wahi na where she was asking, whom do you love?!

Oh! that one.

Actually Shreya it will be awkward but I Love You the most.

How do you know this Zayn?

I realized that I am in love with you and the proof is that I find you everywhere and I can feel you.

Zayn!!! Can I say something? Shreya asked.

Zayn replied-Yeah sure!

I am in love already.

Who is that? Zayn asked in a feeling of losing Shreya.

Shreya Replied – I'm in Love with You …

You are my lifeline and I will never lose you.

Zayn hugged her and then give a kiss on her forehead…

When you are in love with someone, you cannot feel for any other person.

INDEX

Fight with Myself

Truly, for a long time,

I am not happy with myself.

I haven't done any work so far,

Which made me happy with myself.

You say I know nothing; I know everything.

I didn't understand you; I made this mistake.

I want you in my Life, for God's Sake.

I thought,

I would forget you after drinking something.

I miss you by drinking too,

I know who you are, I know everything.

Anyway,

Bae! You are also right in your place,

Nobody will be like me.

Those who clap in front of me,

When I turn abusive me.

Well I know everything. I know everything.

Ashutosh Sharma.

Value

There is a

Difference between

Getting liked and

Getting valued.

Many of them will like,

But very few of them

Value you.

Hence stay with them,

The ones who give value to you.

Abha Bindal

AN UNSUNG MEMORY OF MY LIFE

There was a time when I used to laugh from the inner core my
heart.
There was a time when I was enjoying every small moment of
my life.
There was a time when I used to talk to my friends for more than
an hour and never got bored.
There was a time I used to cry at little things.
There was a time I used to show the smallest pain of my life as
the hardest one to handle.
There was a time I was getting the love back with the same zeal
as I was giving to others.
There was a time when I was not even thinking about my career.
Yes, the time has changed!
Rotation of the time wheel looks even more faster than before.
Now I can't even smile like that…
Yes, I can't even enjoy great moments of my life.
I never ever cry even if I am deeply hurt.
I don't want to show the pain to others as I know nowadays
people start enjoying it rather than standing by my side.
Now I don't even expect to be loved.
I'll make myself understand that I am enough for myself.
Yes, I have no more friends now, but I am happy because I am
not fake.
I am fighting alone and busy in making myself well established.
Closing my eyes and opening the doors…
Time has taught that nobody is yours.

Akanchha Kumari

Shiver

"Are you serious?" he asked "You're already ready to leave? Won't you try to fix this?" She stood there silent, looking down at her feet while tears started forming in her eyes making her sight blurry and in a second or two, they started to fall on her tinted cheeks.

"I-...", she started. She knew that she had to say something. Even if it was just a 'sorry' but she had to. "SAY SOMETHING!", he yelled, his voice a little shaky. He too was on the verge of tears.

He had yelled a few times before in their fights, but this time she was standing in front of him with an answer she couldn't phrase. How do you tell someone that you want to stay and leave at the same time?

"Please... just say something", he begged "do you really want to let this go after all that we've been through?" His eyes always had this glitter in them but today they were sad showing that he was falling apart. He couldn't watch her go. She was still his homeland, his whole world.

She looked in his eyes, struggling with her answer. He could see how hard she was trying to hold back her tears. Oh, if only he could read her mind, but how could he? She had closed the book which he could read easily. She wanted him to know that it was The End. But every word he spoke made her doubt her decision.

"Pilar.... hey. Are you really ready to go?", he once again asked, now the tears in his eyes had made their way out. And just like that what once was a "yes" turned into a "no". "No, not yet", she said.

With tears had started to rolling down her face and words hardly coming out of her soft, tinted shivering lips, she started— her voice just a little above a whisper, "you're a piece of my life now. And if I leave you behind, I know I'll be incomplete, almost empty for the rest of my life."

a.s.

Girl With A Broken Heart

It stained her heart a bit more red

With the wine which spilled,

From the glass, broken and dead,

The same as her heart, shattered and killed.

The nights have witnessed

Her holy tears,

Dripping down her chin,

Drunken by lips and fears,

Being stabbed by her own kith and kin.

The rays of Sun seemed to burn

Her sombre face,

Gleaming bright but dulled by sobriety,

Yet embraced by her grace,

To keep herself safe from society.

Arpita Sahoo

Her Broken Soul

We both were in love, we both were together,

We both wanted each other,

We both knew each other,

One day along with lot of happiness we fought, we fought like

never before, that day onwards endless talks started to become

less,

Our cares became less,

We both were left with lack of words

We both were drifting apart, she tried to resolve but nothing

happened. As he doesn't want them together again.

She was the broken soul with lot of pain and sorrow.

Asmita Ahuja

Abortion

I have undergone an abortion.

Oh God! Will people understand my perception?

Will I be tagged as a selfish, career freak and ruthless mother?

Or they will try to understand my situation?

Misleading in terms, misbehaving of people.

A mother got stuck on the edge of a needle.

No one really cares that even she craves for the love.

The only thing she gets is hatred and shove.

Devyani Neral

A Girl With A Broken Heart

She was sad, torn apart,

She cried for those who were never hers,

She gave pain to herself for those who never felt her pain,

She sacrificed herself for those who never understood her,

She had no one who could stand for her,

She was shattered, broken into pieces,

She was all alone, she had no one,

She was a girl with broken heart …

Dhruvi Dhariwal

Nightmare

Like burning flames of high connotations getting into a notch,

A whisper comes and tells me that this isn't tangible,

I try to run as quick as I can, but that spirit keeps pulling me

closer.

I see the firing of fascinating spirituals,

But my heart kept pounding as if I had lost my worth.

I try to walk and go away,

But the burden is making me stop myself.

These fiery eyes looking precisely from the windows

Are scaring me to get off my bed.

This may be a trap of fondness,

You are making me lose my mind.

I say

"Mom come here! Something is staring at me",

She said "Keep quiet it must be a dream"

I lost words then in fear of getting caught

I stepped out of bed so I could stop it all

My eyes are wide open with fear in my heart

My heart thumping right from the core

I may learn now how to overcome this eerie illusion.

Dua Siddiqui

ME AND MY BROKEN HEART

Under the trees,

I was seated,

Seeing the sky was fully dark,

I was halfly muted.

Someone came from behind,

And that was he,

I thought as he was there to felt sorry,

But, that time he was the only enemy of me.

I hugged him tightly,

And he had his hand in his pocket,

He picked out the knife from his pocket,

I saw, but still waited for him to kill me.

He stopped me,

I was in pain, shouting,

But no one was there who could help me.

He was one,

Who first broke my heart,

And then killed me.

I was shouting,

And 'Me and My Broken Heart' were buried there.

Falha Khan

A WISH TO HEAL

The colourless drops that fall from sky
And the endless stars that twinkle far away
Are her best friends everyday
To whom she cries at night silently
In the whispers of cosmos eternity.
Her grumpy looks in the morning
And silent giggling in the evening
Are all phantom makeup that she wears
To cover the tears that's rolling
Deeper in her heart's covering
Beyond her ephemeral annoyance.
She is something that no one knows
Breathing hard like a caged bird
Praying to fly far from this little abode
Which always gave her the fruits of dolour
Amidst the canyon of her sufferings
To reach that far away panacea
She is trying to heal up harder
And love herself a little deeper
Everyday better than yesterday's chapter.

Gaddam. Nagavaishnavi

Best Birthday Gift Ever

It was my birthday and I was very happy and overwhelmed with happiness...!! I received a lot of text messages and calls from all my friends...!!

But I was waiting for that one person to call me...!!

Suddenly, a notification popped up on my screen and I checked. It was the message from him, "Happy Birthday..!! "I was completely overwhelmed, and I thought now he would call me and make me feel special as always!

Unfortunately, I didn't receive any call that day but at 11.58 p.m. I received a text from him that said, "I can't do this anymore, I want break up with you. We are done!"

My hands started shivering, I wasn't able to control my tears. The moment I heard this, every muscle, every bone in my body broke into pieces.

This was the best gift from my most beloved person! I texted him.

I guess these 2 years of relationship was only one-sided love. I was loving him so much that he started taking me for granted! My one-sided love was left incomplete...!! After that we never called or texted each other.

Garima Jain

I'm A Complicated Person

But honestly, I'm worth all the trouble. Not everyone can understand me, but the people who try to do, they know the kind of person I am. They know me inside out.

When I get attached, I open my heart for people, I overshare my life, I talk without any filter. And then I overthink about the littlest thing of that conversation.

I regret telling them everything. I wonder if they feel for me the way I feel for them. My mind becomes like a crazy monster stuck between chaos and peace.

I don't have a long list of wishes in life. Sometimes, all I want is to be around my people and spend time with them. And during others, I just want to be alone.

Somedays, I feel happy and I want to dance to enjoy that moment. And on other hand, I feel exhausted for no reason. I feel so lost and alone and broken and what not.

Yes, this is me. That's how I am. Simple yet messy, nothing in between, I'm not a bad person trust me. I've just been through more than I could even handle.

I'm a sweetheart for the right person, the one who treats me the way they should and knows my importance in their life.

But I'm a badass for the who take me for granted. For the wrong people who hurt me and the who have cheated on my faith by badly breaking my trust.

Govind M Waswani

She Still Loves

She is girl with a broken heart,

But yes, she still loves,

Why?

Because she knows the pain she had felt, she knows how much it

hurts, when you love someone, and he/she doesn't love you

back!

She is still kind,

But not blind,

She still shines and will always,

She is thankful and grateful for that person who broke her heart,

Only because of that she is kind today, she shines more today!

She considers that heartbreak,

As a blessing in disguise,

She loves the skies,

Yes, she is heartbroken

That's why she is still in love.

Harsha R Gehlani

CHANGE

Change, not for them,

But for yourself.

Change, only if you feel

It's making you exemplary.

Change, not when you can

But when you must.

Change, only when your

Body desires.

Change, only when you're

Ready to change.

Change, only if it doesn't

Change YOU.

The idea of YOU shall remain.

Change, because it's

More than just a part of life.

Change can give you

A more livable life.

Hoshita Sharma

TEARS

Some tears are;

Triggered in the sin of bloodshed,

Flickering of the gunshots,

Weeping many souls in between,

Perplexed by those repercussions,

Some wrenched to be lunatic,

Amidst of that chaos,

Fervor of Regret crawling over me,

Shrieks of those helpless kids,

Carvings of those brutality,

Bestowed condolence to them,

Ambling through those shadows.

Hridhya Manoj

IGNORANT LOVE

Ignore her,

Avoid her,

Also make her feel worthless.

But once she's miffed,

She'll be gone forever.

No matter how hard you try to get her back,

She'll not be there anymore,

Standing by your side,

Holding your hand,

Or giving you hugs.

Thereby hold on to her before she's gone,

And gift her your time,

As that's all she wants.

Jharnashree Deka

Polaris

Poetically praised since times unknown, epitomized as a lover,

With the hope of illuminating the murky nights all long for the

companionship of the moon…

Not among all, I do see its fallacious love, having witnessed its

changing faces

And its absence at nights.

With its borrowed incandescence

It casts a shadow over the one who truly shines.

So,

Don't be the Moon to my night changing faces with time.

Be my stalwart, be my Polaris

And then I'll know you are truly mine.

Kamakshi Verma

Half Finished Letters

A boy and a girl were best friends and that girl was very special for him. She loved him but she hadn't told him, and that boy in love with another girl. Her best friend spends a lot of time with her and one day she decided to write a letter for that boy. Every day she included some special moments spend with him in that letter.

And one day, in afternoon she went to class and was thinking about that boy only. One of her friends asked that "What are you thinking dude?" she decided to share everything with her friend, and she told all her about that boy and all their memories.

Another day her friend went to that boy and said that "Your best friend loves you too much". At the same moment, that boy called her best friend. After a few minutes , she came and asked, "What happened?". He replied that "Your friend told me all about you, that you love me." They both were looking into each other's eyes. Boy told his best friend that he also loved someone. Girl asked, "Whom do you love?". He said, "Your friend who told me all about you".

At that time, she felt too bad and that letter which she had written for boy will always remain half now!!

Krishna Motwani

Hold Your Heart

Life is full of tussle,

You may see me struggle,

But you won't see me fall,

Even in the huge downfall.

Regardless if I'm weak or not,

I'm going to stand tall.

Everyone says life is easy,

Full of roads breezy,

But truly living it is not.

Times get hard, but hold ur heart

People struggle

And constantly get put on the spot.

I'm going to wear the biggest smile,

Even though I want to cry,

I will not quit instead I will try.

I'm going to fight to live,

Even though I'm destined to die.

And even though it's hard

And I may struggle through it all,

You may see me struggle…

But you will NEVER see me fall,

Even in the huge downfall.

Krishna Tiwari

TEARS OF A BROKENHEART

The pain comes out in the form of tears,

Which you can't disclose

Reflecting our anxiety and fear,

The wind of regret blows.

Crying doesn't reflect our weakness,

Inner strength it shows

Smile Shows my Loneliness,

Tears come like a blooming rose.

Clouds of thunder, pouring rain,

The hurt I feel, the throbbing pain

Droplets trickling down my face,

Shall rain give me this one embrace.

Open your heart and cry out loud,

It's time for your ache to shout

We all suffer falls and climbs,

It's okay to cry sometimes.

Kriti Bhatia

Maybe

Stay, I have questions to ask,

You left me at the aisle

Why were you wearing a lover's mask?

If I wasn't good enough to be with

Why were you still there?

You could have left you had your charter

I know it's hard,

I know it's not you but me from the start.

Take my heart and fill your cart.

You'll come again,

To break another piece of my heart.

See I'll give all your shots,

But can you love me once

And not pretend to be my part.

I know it's hard

Baby, you have aces,

But remember I even don't lack cards.

Maybe I am not done,

Maybe I still think you are the one,

You have broken me.

It's been a while you haven't spoken to me.

I guess you have moved on,

Or maybe waiting for my word.

Maybe I am mad,

But you can come back anytime you want.

Maybe it's just me here alone,

Maybe I am asking for what's not mine at all.

It's ok to be apart,

Maybe this is my new start.

Laya Shree

FIRST MEMORY OF MY LOVE

My Love,

I still have your rose

Which is the symbol of our love

Now it's a symbol of my pain

All of a sudden, you vanished.

Instead of filling happy tears in my eyes, you filled sad tears!

Instead of filling my heart with your love, you filled pain!

Yes, but even then I am still ok.

Because you left me, but your rose which defines our love never

left me and it still gives hope on our Love, that one day you will

come back to me with a Marriage proposal.

Dear old love,

Thank you so much for leaving me.

Because I realised that you are not worth to have my love And In

future, someone deserves my Love who treat me as if am a

Queen to their Kingdom, called Life.

Mallela Ravikumar Jayasudha

Unexplained You

I put the nib of my pen on the paper

And in a blink, everything went blank

I closed my eyes and I tried again

But again, I penned nothing but a dot.

I reversed my thoughts

Thought of what to write

Write about you- just you.

But then, I realized

I can never write you

You are not bounded to be in words

But live in my mind and heart.

Meenakshi

Broken Heart

He starts avoiding her,
She feels broken hearted.
He stops talking towards her,
She feels broken hearted.
He starts distancing with her,
She feels broken hearted.
He stops smiling at her,
She feels broken hearted.
He said I am hopeless,
She feels broken hearted,
He is not messaging her,
She feels broken hearted.
He is not replying for her message,
She feels broken hearted.
He is angry with her,
She feels broken hearted.
He said I am not trusting you,
She feels broken hearted.
He is not ready to convey with her,
She feels broken hearted.
He is not willing for compromise,
She feels broken hearted.
He is not taking the call,
She feels broken hearted.
He finally blocked her,
She feels broken hearted.

Nesba Sahir

Self Acceptance

I wish to paint my body

With the colours I lack,

I point out each one of my flaws,

And sideline my every perfection,

As if I'm always searching

For a reason to degrade myself.

I'm all in when it comes to lecture

About self-love,

But seldom do I practice it.

I can go on and on,

Writing about self-acceptance,

Only for it to be trapped forever,

Amongst my ceaseless self-loathing.

I never thought that one day,

Living in my own body

Would feel like a task to me.

How can I ever expect to top your priority list?

When I always come last on mine?

Nitya Aggarwal

A girl with a broken heart

A girl that was still trying to live

But not she is struggling to breathe.

Benevolent and warm she was but now laying on the edge of the

iced gouge.

Sincerity rooted deeply in her mind but now poisoned with lies

as time went by.

She handed out her heart but was returned with arrows from the

attacks.

All she asked for was love only if she knew it was cursed.

How does she live from here?

Does she build up iron walls to be fierce?

How does she write from here?

Will she continue to use her blood as ink and tears?

How does she listen from here?

Will she drown the voices or live with her fears?

She was a girl with so much love and light but now she is just a

girl with a broken heart.

Odighizuwa patience lilaz

YOURS DISASTER LANDFALL

Crave me at the verge of your craze.

Well it's your ultimate stage

No sorry no marriage.

Miss me at the spot of your sin:

And then I'll escape with a tin.

No, I ain't your crime queen.

Feel me at the sense of your pain

Similarly drowning like your tears drain.

Not again, I'm not your rain.

Screams of your soul seeking for my call

Well I'm not even toy to play like a ball:

Yes, I'm yours disaster landfall.

Don't mistake me as your fault.

I'm the one with no halt:

A mere outcome of thy jolt.

Pragyan Panda

A Toxic Relationship

How do you know that relying on person till lifetime will
blossom up??
How does it feel when you are the only one putting in constant
efforts in a relation as if only it matters to you as if only you
want it to last!! Feels disheartened right??
I still keep wondering how people seem so okay with themselves
knowing that they have destroyed someone emotionally!!!
How can someone be so calm with all those negative and awful
behaviour of theirs towards someone who loves them!!
Ahh!! This is so toxic!!
What if they come back over and over to tell you sorry about it
and you forgive it every possible time.
Now wait forgiveness is given to those who commit a mistake
not for a continuous behaviour.
A person in relation from years & years knows you from the tip
of hairs to bottom of toe comes back with apology for their
constant behavior which intentionally is done to cause hurt to
you!!
Mistake is something we make once or twice but when the
mistake is made more than twice hold on now it's a "CHOICE".
Choices are to be forgiven but not forgotten.
So, walk out.. Walk out before you emotionally, mentally drain
proving yourself correct. Walk out before your mind starts
controlling your body. Walk out before you forget your worth &
beauty.
Burn all those emotions, walk free and change because it's never
too late!!

RANI BALKRISHNA YADAV

PROMISE

"I promise to hold your hands forever'

I promise to be with you

In the days of high tide and delight."

All these false speeches,

Your spurious, your honourable words.

Every time you come up with new promise

And the next moment you show deeper hue.

Ages passed same as your promise

But the only constant are your deceitful promises.

Now it's scary for me to gulp down your false words.

I don't want any promises further,

Just leave me alone in my world.

Ritu Jha

Falling for her again

Falling for her again was not easy

What happened in the past was a lot breezy

I didn't get the love I deserved so I was greedy

So eventually I had to pretend like a needy

After some time, conversations with her also got cheesy

We got connected well and it was being crazy

Life again flowed well as being greasy

Life again smelled so good like that daisy

But smell doesn't last, and life again got lazy

She started being weird and always being busy

The time it hit me that I don't belong to that specie

And just made my life to hazy

So, decided to make my life alone that crazy

And this reminds me falling for her again was not easy…..

Rupal Khemani

RESPECT WOMEN

Respect is the Desire of everybody's mind,
But is only given to people who are kind.
Respect is given to those who deserve it,
And not to those who betray for it.
Respect is like a fuel for life,
Without which a man cannot drive!
Respect to our elders plays an important role,
As it's the blessing to achieve our goal.
Respect is like the bullet of a gun,
Which Travels with us in long run.
Respect when given to all,
His reputation will never fall.
Women exist as a daughter, a sister, a mother, or a wife,
Without her support, contribution, and selfless work a man
cannot work rife.
There is no fun to wait for others to motivate,
Discrimination must be kept out of gate.
We humans have to change our mentality,
Men, women as well as others should be considered equal as
natural, what God has sent us is the reality.

Sahaj Sabharwal

My Untold Story

As I was walking through the dark lane,

I could feel my every pain,

From the brewing present to the startled past,

All those emotions went into vain.

Those scary shadows of pain,

Which my past has gained,

Carves every inch of my body,

And I have no one to sooth.

All I was drowning,

In the ocean of meaningless empathy,

There you came like the spectrum from heaven.

Just like a diver who saved me from hell.

You became my happiness,

Even in my subconsciousness.

Collecting all those shattered pieces of mine,

You started healing them with all your love wine.

To the face without smile,

You taught them how to glow,

To those weak feet,

You made them stronger,

Not just to walk for a while but for mile.

To those eyes with tears,

You removed all their fears.

To those weak hands,

You made them bulldozer.

You were just not a chapter of my book,

Rather a whole summary of my life.

You became my happiness

With millions of reasons to go ahead.

Samikhya Swain (Ikhya)

MANIFESTING YOU.

All my energy is you,

The smell I love,

Voice I hear,

Aura I feel,

Even I dream of our love life..

Knowing the source inside me will make it true.

Oh, my soulmate, my entire energy is tending towards you,

Visualizing our life…..love life..

Vibrating my desires..

Never anticipating or expecting to know when..

For I know..

You are mine.. my soul's whole..

Universe promised, me..

That I am manifesting you..

Will never be apart, and the love with us will grows a lot.

Shalinisurya

A Girl With A Repaired Heart

Once upon a time on the highlands grass,

There lived a girl, named Chloe.

She was a storm, hard to stop

She fell in love with a man of treachery.

Then a storm, now just a snowflake

Broken into pieces and started living with the cliches.

She tried to fix her heart with a glue of love

And tried to replace the pains with colourful hues.

To her, love becomes an impossible thing until the time Lucifer

came in.

He put her pieces back together and made it a new one.

Her tears turned into laughter, and aches in joys.

A broken heart can still be fixed, by the one who knows how to

do it.

Sharmistha Kar

THE MOURNING

He murmured, I heard,

Words were quite similar,

It was like every single word,

As if I heard them earlier.

During the mourning period,

I heard him saying something,

I felt a touch over my hand,

Those airy words while mourning.

The air crossed my ears,

He said, "don't you miss us?"

I looked back with fear,

But I saw only girls.

The voice was obviously, of a man,

Even though I found no man near me,

Who might it be then?

Obviously, he could be.

I thought it was just a feeling,

But then again he said,

"You look ugly while crying."

How could I listen him even after being dead?

Did he really miss me that much?

That even came to see me,

If me, too, could reach,

I would have said all those words but now it can't be.

Shikha Malik

HER SHATTERED FEELING

The very known thing, which is unknown by ages,
Girl who wears a smile has a heart broken.
From chirping of bird to twinkling of star,
A happy soul always thought what was her scar,
With a rainbow in sky & blooming floret she felt her pumping
blood,
When she broke down & ceased her hope all she left with
dripping soul.
Her heart is now in so much pain,
Her tears are falling like steady rain,
No one can save her from the dark's might,
This time there will be no light.
She can no longer sleep a full night,
She can no longer fight,
Because she is broken this much from inside,
Again, she can't stand for her MR. RIGHT.
She never did show how she felt,
Just believe me,
Every time she saw you,
Her heart used to melt.
The very known thing, which is unknown by ages,
Girl who seems to be strong has a heart broken.

Shreya Gupta

The Pride : A Daughter

What's stopping you?

Feel free to do,

You are not someone's property,

You can do things with liberty.

You are a daughter of your family,

Who needs to live merrily and happily,

Without any tensions or chaos,

Or with any fear of loss?

You are an epitome of the society,

Someone with full of beauty,

Who does her work faithfully,

And cannot be repudiate easily.

Do your work with responsibility

Always be calm and gently,

Because you are the pride,

Who should be always exemplified?

Simi Chutia

Broken Nights

The undeciphered tales of the worthy mind,
Clashed against a sore and broken heart.
The night at its peak stood ravishing,
Peeking through the windshield of a
Perfectly lit moon and curious leaves,
A curtain of cold breeze failed to keep
My indecisive self from its real judgements.
I tried to swim across the ocean of clouds
Only to reach out to the temple of truths.
The chirps continued from a distant tree,
Amplified by the intoxicated serenity of
That anxiously long night, I sighed.
Shadows kept coming from the depths
And lights seemed to descend from the heavens,
I was pulled offshore, the waves of moonlight
Loved me more than those everlasting lies,
Utterly infernal darkness wooed me secretly
And my trembling feet traversed the viscous
Yet numbing paths of the witching-hour.
Oh, so glad was I, discovering those textured
Areas of darkness, for once I was free,
My mind unrivaled and certain for moments,
Thoughts impenetrable and viciously appealing,
My heart never skipped a beat, joyous but vile.
Those hours, smeared with concealed facts,
My subconscious was clear and pure for once,

They said it's overthinking, all in my head,

But the devil admired it attentively, with a smirk.

Late nights picturised a perfectly clear time,

The nyctophile in me was born under the stars,

While the moon and the clouds added to its

Eternally attractive beauty, auspicious and dim.

The stories inside my "unworthy" titled heart

Are jumbled and twisted.

It lures me towards the shining and blinding

Lights, while I still crave for those dark valleys.

That glow tried harder and harder, to lead me,

Into the whole new universe of happiness,

I'm afraid, shy, solitary, rude, played,

Anxious and broken, I tend to retreat

Into the wells of sorrow again, for my heart was crushed, oh so

bad!

Should I take the risky walk or just stand back?

"You're worthy of every happiness this world

Has to offer", screamed the voices inside my head.

I lift up my chin every time it drops, the flowers

Bring me crowns, for I'm brave, respectable,

Honest, true, fierce, and strong.

I walk down the path.

Simran Dhingra

Lost love

Broken soul!

In spite of me, giving everything, we wanted,

Unknowingly, a hole chasm through me,

Like the one, my father did to the silver mug,

While throwing it in our depository.

A deep hole-seemingly incurable.

Later, you poured out all your love,

Yet, I couldn't keep, even the least with me.

I cried and my tears vanished through the hole.

I stored my feelings and they evaporated soon.

You neither had a fault nor I have.

I tried my hard to recover,

You had put some balms too,

Nonetheless, during all these things,

Perhaps, I lost everything.

You!

Your love!

And yes, my existence!

Subhrajyoti Nanda

HEART IS BROKEN BUT THERE'S A WORLD TO LIVE

My heart is broken, and I have lost everything. The world is upset with me, God is unreal. He took away from me. I roamed door to door all over the places, but my beloved couldn't be found. OH! Beloved person why you leave me with teary eyes, with a unfulfilled dream. Someone console me; with the knowledge that you are playing with my emotions, but I don't believe them, because have trust on You. But you have betrayed that on your own hand. The saints have written so much about love. But still I don't get what love is for me!! Because you left me with teary eyes

Why is life, just a moment or two?

For this love, centuries are not enough..

So, let me ask God

For some more time, anew,

I have to live just here,

I have not to go away from you..

Now that you are there to share my pain,

Now that you share my pain,

Every pain is beautiful,

Now that I can manage my pain because there is something for which I must live and it's my FAMILY. Your smiles are my strength.

I got hope from them only.

Whatever atrocity the world does to me,

In them [these smiles] is my safety.

My life became very beautiful with you. But now a time I want rebuild the daylight with fresh start. Why should this heart remain lonely?

Why should we live in pieces.?

Why should my soul bear this.?

I've been living alone..
I'm saying this every moment,
That I need you..

That I need you….. But you are not there for me. It's so hard to forget pain, but it's even harder to remember sweetness. We have no scar to show for happiness. We learn so little from peace. To give so much time to the improvement of yourself. That you have no time to criticize others. To be too large for worry, too noble for anger, too strong for fear,

And too happy to permit the presence of trouble. I will try to relieve myself with a new daylight and start a new journey to Fly.

Swalna S. Tripathy

If Only

If only I could lacerate these,

Layers of lamentations –

That remained etched on my essay,

Without having to –

Relinquish the remnants of yours,

For these were –

And had always been both the cause,

And the cure –

Of that every adoringly abhorred,

Rue of mine.

Tabassum Hasnat

The fear of losing you

As I lay in bed thinking of you,
Helpless in your thoughts not knowing what to do.
I try to feel the warmth of you,
And oh, so comfortable I'm with you.
So far you are yet so near,
You are the exact reason I'm here.
I await the times when we can talk,
I await the times when together we can walk.
To feel you near me,
The happiest person I'd ever be.
You've always sent me reminder,
That you'll always make me shine brighter.
You, being mine, I still lose my mind,
Coz you'll always be one of a kind.
When someone gets close to you,
Jealousy takes a darker hue.
Why without you am I so blue?
Why do I have this fear of losing you?

Terrina Fernandes

INVISIBLE WOUNDS

This pain never ends,
This feeling is constant.
I see nothing but darkness,
I get nothing but suffering.
This thing is breaking my body,
One by one,
My stomach hurts,
My bones are cracking,
My body is cold.
Sleep haunts me,
People in my dreams kill me,
I wake up with a heavy heart
And teary eyes.
I try not to sleep,
But when it hurts my eyes,
I cannot stop.
"One breath at a time"
I say to myself.
But what if I breathe in.
And never breathe out?
I'm not afraid of death.
I'm afraid of the continuous,
Pain and sufferings that never end.
I'm afraid of the questions ,
I never get answers of…

Vaishali Bindal

The Pain Behind My Smile

I am standing here by the shore,

With a broken heart,

With a mixed feeling,

Tears rolling down my cheeks,

Hoping that it would melt away my pain.

I am lost in this path,

Failures, rejections numb my heart,

I am losing trust in my loved ones,

I fool them with my smile,

Because I have nothing left to feel.

Surrounded by people,

But none could see the pain in my eyes,

I wished,

I had someone to pull me out from this darkness,

Show me the light in this blurred life path.

They came,

And they left me drowning in this pain,

I continued to smile again.

Vanmitha Athimoolam

BLEEDING THORNS

I reminisced

About the roses I painted

On our beating hearts,

While lying on the floor of my bedroom

Feeling numb, anesthetized

In the drought.

Beneath my eyes.

You took the roses

To send demons into my tower,

Throbbing and excruciating my skin,

I bled with thorns,

Hidden in my roses.

Void

दिल के दरमियान

कुछ प्यारे से ख़्वाब देखे थे उनके साथ ,

जिसने सिर्फ़ हमसे प्यार किया था ,

ज़िंदगी इतनी रंगीन होकर भी बेरंग हो गयी ,

तुम्हारी ज़िंदगी में ना हो के भी हमने कब्ज़ा कर लिया तुमपे ,

लोगो के इतने चेहरे होते है ये आज खुद का दूसरा चेहरा देख ,

पता चला ।

रोना तो ज़रूर चाहा था लेकिन खुश भी उतनी ही हूँ,

क्योंकि तुमने आखिर मुझे भुला अपना दूसरा रूप देखा।

ये दिखाना आसान हैं पर जताना मुश्किल की हाँ हमने सिर्फ़ तुमसे

प्यार किया था,

लेकिन मौहोल ओर हालात के दरमियान प्यार से बड़ी इज़्ज़त हो

गयी,

तुम्हारा नाम लेने से पहले मुझे पालने वाले का नाम संभालना सही

समझा,

हाँ क्योंकि यही वजह थी कि तुम्हें भी मेरा दूसरा रूप देखने

मिल गया।

Bhavini dhuva

इश्क़ था उससे

इश्क़ हुआ था उससे,

वो मज़ाक नहीं था।

दुनिया जानती थी ,

कोई राज़ नहीं था।

प्यार माँग था मैने ,

पर उसने तो साथ भी छोड़ दिया।

मेरी हर चीज़ उसपे कुर्बान थी,

लेकिन उसके लिए तो कोई और उसकी जान थी।

हाँ नहीं है वो आज मेरे साथ,

पर क्या हुआ उसका एहसास तो आज भी मेरे पास है।

तोड़ दिया उसने मेरा दिल कुछ इस क़दर,

जैसे कोई पुराना शीशा था,

हाँ इश्क़ हुआ था मुझे ,

वो कोई मज़ाक नहीं था।

Chavi Mehra

ऐहसास- टूटने का और जिंदा रहने की चाह

रातों के अंधेरों से अब वो डरा नहीं करती
बंदिशों की बेड़ियों से खुद को जकड़ा नहीं करती,
बनना चाहती हैं जो टूटने के बाद भी चमकता हुआ तारा
ए! कठोर दिल जमाने वो स्त्री बार – बार जन्मा नहीं करती।
कहती है बुरा भला ये, धोखेबाज दुनिया, तो कहने दो इसे
क्योंकि कुछ तो लोग कहेंगे , लोगो का काम है कहना।
टूटी हुई इमारत की कीमत भी मकान बनने के बाद ही बढ़ती है
मेरी कीमत भी मेरे बिखरे हुए टुकड़ों को जोड़ने के बाद ही
समझेगा ये जमाना,
इसलिए बोलना इनकी आदत
और माफ़ करना फिलहाल मेरी जरूरत है।
हकीक़त को बदलने की कामना रखने वाली
अपनी हिम्मत और हौसले पर विश्वास रखने वाली,
कठिन कसौटियों को पार कर जाने वाली
अपनी मंज़िल से जुदा हुआ नहीं करती।
मुंह फेर लेते है वो जो कभी हमें अपना सग्गा कहा करते थे,
पैगाम तो दुःख में अपने भी भेजा नहीं करते
हंसते – हंसते उस दर्द के विष को पी जाने के बाद भी
जिंदा रहने की चाहत रखने वाली।
इतिहास के पन्नों की मशहूर रचना बना करती हैं
लेकिन आम मौत मरा नहीं करती।

Chinsha Bhatia

Poora Hokar Bhi Adhoora

Seekh liya apni feelings ko control karna. Seekh liya tere bina jeena. Seekh liya teri har ek baat ko yaad karke roona. Seekh liya ab teri yaadon mein panaah hona. Tere saath jeena tha par shayad khuda ne ye chaha nai tha. Tujhe har ek baat bataya karti thi. Rote wakt tera kanda hamesha saath hota tha. Darkar teri baahon me lipta karti thi mein. Tujhe sabse jyada chaha tha, par ab tu hi nahi!

Kuch galat ho jaye mere saath toh tere gale lag jaaya karti thi. Sabke saamne tera haath thama karti thi. Kyuki tujhse saccha pyar jo karti thi. Socha tha ki saath nibaega tu hamesha par ki toone khafa. Mujhe pata hai kuch toh galat kiya hai maine jo tu mujhe chorh kar chala gaya. Par ab toh maaf karde. Ek baar apni pehle waali jaan ko apna le.

Diksha Motwani

अधूरी ख्वाहिश

मिल जाय मुझे वो किसी मोड़ पर ख़ुदा से ये गुज़ारिश थी!
पर ये हो ना सका मगर उसके अलावा और किसी की ना फरमाइश
थी!
पा न सका उसको मे उम्र बीत गयी इंतज़ार में उसके
उसको पाना मेरी ज़िंदगी की अधूरी ख्वाहिशें थी!
मिले शायद किसी मोड़ पर हम दोनों और फिर बिछड़े ना कभी हो
जाय काश ऐसा!
क्योंकि हैं नहीं कोई इस दुनिया मे मेरे दिल के करीब उस जैसा!
जब साथ थे, हम तब जिंदगी मेरी गुलज़ार थी !
पूछो अगर मुझसे के किसका नाम हैं, जुबां पे मेरे तो मेरी जुबां पे वो
ही हर बार थी!
की थी मोहब्बत इतनी के हो जाती कभी-कभी हम में तकरार थी!
फ़िर मनाने की बारी मेरी उसको हर बार थी
क्योंकि मोहब्बत मेरे सर पे जो सवार थी!
गयी हैं जबसे छोड़ के, आगये मुझपर सितम हैं
अब रूठने मनाने का किस्सा भी ख्तम है!
काश! वो आ जाती वापिस हर पल खुशियाँ भरा होता
निहारता रहता उसको फिर मैं नहीं उस रात सोता,
आ जाये वापिस फ़िर से किससे करूँ सिफारिश?
करना बहुत कुछ हैं, उसके लिए मगर रह गयी मेरी वो सब करने
की अधूरी ख्वाहिश

Kalamkaar

ना वो आया, ना ख़बर उसकी

आँखों ही आँखों में सारी रात कट गई,
ना नींद ही आयी, ना ही कोई ख़बर उसकी।
तकती रही दरवाज़े को टकटकी लगाए,
हर धड़कन पर लगता आहट है ये उसकी
हवायें जो गुजरती थी छूकर मुझे,
महसूस होती थी खुशबू भीनी भीनी सी उसकी।
पलटती रही पन्ने यादों के रात भर,
कुछ भूली बिसरी बातें याद आई उसकी।
लिखती रही मिटाती रही किस्से बीते वक़्त के,
कुछ नग़मे मेरे प्यार के, कुछ दिल्लगी उसकी।
करवटों में कट गई रात सारी,
आँखों में थी बस झलक उसकी।
साँस लेना भी हो रहा था दूभर,
जैसे मेरी साँसें जुड़ीं हों साँसों से उसकी।
उसके आने का कोई वादा तो न था,
फ़िर भी जाने क्यों निगाहें थी राहों में उसकी।
आँखों के बादल कर रहे थे बारिश,
जाने कैसे सूखी रह गई दिल की जमीं उसकी।
इंतज़ार के लम्हें काटे कट्ते नहीं थे,
जान ले रही थी मेरी, बेरुखी उसकी।
यूँ तो रखता है मुझे सीने से लगाये,
आखिर मैं भी तो 'जान' हूँ उसकी।
फिर भी रात गुज़री उसके इंतज़ार में,
पर आया ना वो, ना ही कोई ख़बर उसकी।

Mridula

यू चले जाने से चाहते नहीं मिटती

हाँ मेरी ये ख़ता है

की कर रहे हैं यकीन तेरे जाने पर भी हम

तुमने तो मुड़ के देखा भी ना था एक बार,

जिसे तुम अपनी मोहब्बत कहकर बुलाया करते थे

ना जाने किस आस में हूँ मैं?

हाँ ये मेरी ख़ता है

की कर रहे हैं यकीन तेरे जाने पर भी हम

आहटे अब बस ख्यालों में ही मिलती है तुम्हारी,

आँख खुलते ही तुमसे दूर होने का एहसास

हर लम्हा ज़हन में मौजूद रहती है मेरी

सुबह की पहली प्याली चाय के साथ

और शाम के ढलते किरणों के साए में,

गुप्तगू तुमसे कुछ यूँ कर लिया करते है हम।

Nishant Kumar

मै मोहब्बत और वो

एक रात मैंने कहा चाँद और तारों से
के मेरी जान अच्छी है फूल की बहारों से
इस पर चाँद भड़क कर बोला:
के जो तूने कहा वो क्या मज़ाक है?
तेरी जान के आगे तो रात के तारे भी ख़ाक है।
उसकी आँखो में शरारत और बातों में बचपना है
उसके सिवा कोई और कहाँ लगता अब अपना है?
तुझे बाहों में भर के अपना बनाके तुझे गले लगना है
तू एक सपना है जिसे अपनी हकीक़त बनाना है,
उसने कहा तुम नहीं मेरे काबिल मुझे भूल जाओ
मैंने ख़ुद और दुनिया को तराजू में रखा तो,
एक तरफ को झूल गया
जब उसने ऐसा कहा था तो कीमत ना पता थी मेरी
इसलिए उसकी इस ख़ता को में भूल गया।
मेरी मोहब्बत उसके शरीर से नहीं है
जो उससे दूर होकर खत्म हो जाएगी
मैंने उसकी रूह को चाहा है,
तो ये मोहब्बत क़यामत साथ जाएगी
ना होकर भी मेरी दुनिया में तुम मुझे रोज़ याद आते हो,
हर रात मेरे सपने में अकेले मुझसे मिलने आते हो
पता नहीं ये दुश्मनी या प्यार है तुम्हारा?
सपने में हँसाते हँसाते असलियत में रुलाते हो।

Nitin

बेवफ़ा नसीब

हर वक़्त हर घड़ी खुदको यूँ मारा करती हूँ

जब तुमको मैं दुबारा याद करती हूँ।

मुझे तालाब रहने दो सबकी प्यास मिटा सकूँ

आखिर समंदर तो सिर्फ़ पानी को खारा करता है।

जिसके नसीब में ही किसी की वफ़ा लिखी नहीं है

वो तो सिर्फ़ शायरी को पन्नों में उतारा करते हैं।

दिल तो पूरी तरह से टूट चुका है

फुरसत मिले तो मुझे पढ़ना ज़रूर,

उसकी बेवफ़ा मोहब्बत की पूरी किताब हूँ।

शब्दों से भरी हुई हूँ मैं पर फिर भी क्यों मौन हूँ मैं।

अब मुझे खोलने की कोशिश करना मत

क्योंकि जो थी मैं अब वो रही नहीं और जो हूँ वो शायद किसीको

पता नहीं।

फिर भी हर वक़्त हर घड़ी खुद को यूँ मारा करती हूँ

जब तुमको मैं दुबारा याद करती हूँ।

Priyanka Panda 'DP'

वो किसी और को सोचता होगा

रात में जब चाँद देखूं तो ये खयाल आये मुझको,

वो भी खड़ा चाँद को ही देखता होगा..

जिस तरह मैं सोच रही तन्हाई में उसको,

व भी मेरे बारे में ही सोचता होगा।

रहना है राह में खोले हुए बांहें,

शायद आ कर मेरी बाहों में वो समा जाए...

होती रहती है मेरे दिल में ऐसी कई उलझन,

वो भी कई उलझनों में उलझता होगा।

फिर खुल जाती है आँखे कुछ यूँ मेरी,

सपनो से आती हूँ में बाहर..

कुछ ये सोचती हूँ फिर!

कि खो ना जाऊँ उसके प्यार की वो खुशबू मैं,

नहीं झेल पाऊँगी वो दर्द,जब टूटेगी ये मोहब्बत...

आज आ पड़ा है...सब बिखरा पड़ा है...

वो दर्द ही है अब मुझे झेलना।

और फिर जब चाँद देखूं तो ये ख्याल आये मुझको

वो भी खड़ा चाँद को ही देखता होगा...

जिस तरह मैं सोच रही तन्हाई में उसको

वो भी किसी और को सोचता होगा।

Srujan Hiral Gaurang

उम्मीदें

मैंने ये बात अब तक किसी से कही नहीं

के उम्मीदें अब किसी से रही नहीं

मंज़िल तक पहुँचने पर भी ,

मंज़िल अब तक मिली नहीं

ये तो कुछ मतलबी लोगो की मेहरबानी है ,

वरना आस तो अभी बुझी नहीं।

ये समय कि घड़ी भी अब यूँ चली

के भरोसे कि छड़ी अब किसी पर रही नहीं

तू भी नादान थी ख्वाबीदा,

के दूसरों को छोड़ ख़ुद के संग कभी चली नहीं।

मैंने ये बात अब तक किसी से कही नहीं

के उम्मीदें अब किसी से रही नहीं

के उम्मीदें अब किसी से रही नहीं।

Zubia Mariyam

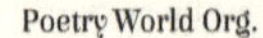